Leaving My Homeland

A Refugee's Journey from
Eritrea

Linda Barghoorn

CRABTREE
PUBLISHING COMPANY
WWW.CRABTREEBOOKS.COM

CRABTREE
PUBLISHING COMPANY
WWW.CRABTREEBOOKS.COM

Author: Linda Barghoorn

Editors: Sarah Eason, Harriet McGregor,
Wendy Scavuzzo, and Janine Deschenes

Proofreader and indexer: Wendy Scavuzzo

Editorial director: Kathy Middleton

Design: Paul Myerscough and Jessica Moon

Cover design: Paul Myerscough and Jessica Moon

Photo research: Rachel Blount

**Production coordinator and
   Prepress technician:** Ken Wright

Print coordinator: Katherine Berti

Consultants: Hawa Sabriye and HaEun Kim, Centre for Refugee Studies,
   York University

Produced for Crabtree Publishing Company by Calcium Creative

Publisher's Note: The story presented in this book is a fictional account
based on extensive research of real-life accounts by refugees, with the aim
of reflecting the true experience of refugee children and their families.

Photo Credits:
t=Top, bl=Bottom Left, br=Bottom Right

Inside: Alamy: Eric Lafforgue: p. 12; Jessica Moon: p. 29bl; Shutterstock:
Best-Backgrounds: pp. 26-27; Brothers Good: p. 6b; Homo Cosmicos:
p. 11b; Edward Crawford: p. 23; Nicolas Economou: p. 22t;
Flamencodiablo Photography: p. 20; Patricia Hofmeester: p. 15tl;
Matej Hudovernik: p. 9t; Inspiring: p. 9b; Jemastock: p. 22bl; JM Travel
Photography: p. 7b; Lana2016: p. 7t; Lawkeeper: p. 29tl; Macrovector:
p. 3; Maiyude: p. 29t; MikeDotta: p. 21c; MSSA: pp. 28t, 29cl; Rvector:
p. 21t; Fredy Thuerig: p. 8b; VectorShow: p. 10b; Vikpoint: p. 8t; What's
My Name: p. 16t; UNHCR: © UNHCR/Andreea Anca: p. 25; © UNHCR/
Fabio Bucciarelli: p. 17cl; © UNHCR/W. Van Bemmel: p. 22b; ©
UNHCR/Frederic Courbet: pp. 15c, 17cr, 18-19c; © UNHCR/Kisut Gebre
Egziabher: p. 13; © UNHCR/Marc Hofer: p. 26b; © UNHCR/Francesco
Malavolta: p. 19b; © UNHCR/E. Parsons: p. 4-5c; © UNHCR/Marcello
Pastonesi: p. 24; Wikimedia Commons: Helene C. Stikkel: p. 10t.

Cover: Jessica Moon; Shutterstock: Prazis Images.

Library and Archives Canada Cataloguing in Publication

Barghoorn, Linda, author
   A refugee's journey from Eritrea / Linda Barghoorn.

(Leaving my homeland)
Includes index.
Issued in print and electronic formats.
ISBN 978-0-7787-4686-7 (hardcover).--
ISBN 978-0-7787-4697-3 (softcover).--
ISBN 978-1-4271-2070-0 (HTML)

   1. Refugees--Eritrea--Juvenile literature. 2. Refugees--Netherlands--
Amsterdam--Juvenile literature. 3. Refugee children--Eritrea--Juvenile
literature. 4. Refugee children--Netherlands--Amsterdam--Juvenile
literature. 5. Refugees--Social conditions--Juvenile literature. 6. Eritrea--
Social conditions--Juvenile literature. I. Title.

HV640.5.E75B37 2018   j305.9'0691409635   C2017-907646-9
                                                 C2017-907647-7

Library of Congress Cataloging-in-Publication Data

Names: Barghoorn, Linda, author.
Title: A refugee's journey from Eritrea / Linda Barghoorn.
Description: New York : Crabtree Publishing, [2018] |
   Series: Leaving my homeland | Include index.
Identifiers: LCCN 2017054807 (print) | LCCN 2017057138 (ebook) |
   ISBN 9781427120700 (Electronic HTML) |
   ISBN 9780778746867 (reinforced library binding : alk. paper) |
   ISBN 9780778746973 (pbk. : alk. paper)
Subjects: LCSH: Refugee children--Eritrea--Juvenile literature. |
   Refugees--Eritrea--Juvenile literature. | Eritrea--Emigration and
   immigration--Juvenile literature.
Classification: LCC HV640.5.A3 (ebook) | LCC HV640.5.A3 B37 2018
   (print) | DDC 305.9/0691409635--dc23
LC record available at https://lccn.loc.gov/2017054807

Crabtree Publishing Company
www.crabtreebooks.com   1-800-387-7650

Printed in the U.S.A./022018/CG20171220

Copyright © **2018 CRABTREE PUBLISHING COMPANY**. All rights reserved. No part of this publication may be reproduced, stored in a retrieval
system or be transmitted in any form or by any means, electronic, mechanical, photocopying, recording, or otherwise, without the prior written
permission of Crabtree Publishing Company. In Canada: We acknowledge the financial support of the Government of Canada through the
Canada Book Fund for our publishing activities.

Published in Canada
Crabtree Publishing
616 Welland Ave.
St. Catharines, Ontario
L2M 5V6

Published in the United States
Crabtree Publishing
PMB 59051
350 Fifth Avenue, 59th Floor
New York, New York 10118

Published in the United Kingdom
Crabtree Publishing
Maritime House
Basin Road North, Hove
BN41 1WR

Published in Australia
Crabtree Publishing
3 Charles Street
Coburg North
VIC, 3058

What Is in This Book?

Leaving Eritrea...4

My Homeland, Eritrea 6

Dawit's Story: Growing Up in Eritrea 8

The Conflict in Eritrea 10

Dawit's Story: Fleeing Eritrea 12

Fleeing the Conflict 14

Dawit's Story: Life in Adi Harush Camp 16

Life in a Refugee Camp 18

Dawit's Story: The Journey to Europe 20

Reaching a New Life in Europe 22

Dawit's Story: Life in the Netherlands............24

Challenges Refugees Face..............................26

You Can Help! 28

Glossary 30

Learning More..31

Index and About the Author............................32

Leaving Eritrea

Many people in Eritrea are very poor. They stay alive by growing the food they need to survive. Sometimes, there is not enough rain in the country for crops to grow. When this happens, many people become sick or die from the lack of food.

The Eritrean government keeps tight control of the country. It does not allow citizens to choose their religion or speak against the government. The country does not have a **constitution**. A constitution is a document that protects peoples' **rights**. Not everyone in Eritrea understands their rights.

Eritrea has mountains along its central section, and lowlands to the east. Asmara is the capital city.

● Asmara

UN Rights of the Child

Every child has rights. Rights are privileges and freedoms that are protected by law. **Refugees** have the right to special protection and help. The **United Nations (UN)** Convention on the Rights of the Child is a document that lists the rights of children all over the world. Think about these rights as you read this book.

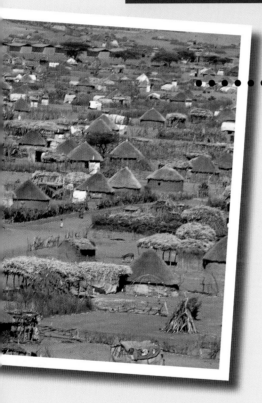

The houses in this village in western Eritrea have mud walls and thatched roofs.

The Eritrean government says it needs a large, strong army. It wants to defend itself from its neighbor, Ethiopia. To build its army, it forces every student to do **military service** before finishing high school. They must serve at least 1.5 years, but sometimes they serve 10 years or more.

To escape **poverty**, violence, and lack of freedom, thousands of Eritreans have fled their **homeland** and have become refugees. Refugees are people who fled their homeland because of war and other unsafe conditions. Refugees are different from **immigrants**. Immigrants chose to leave to look for better opportunities in another country.

My Homeland, Eritrea

Eritrea is one of the poorest countries on Earth. It had a long war with Ethiopia that lasted 30 years. It became **independent** from Ethiopia in 1993. Today, 5.9 million people live in Eritrea. More than 75 percent of them live in the countryside. Many people in Eritrea move around instead of living in one place. They do this to find good land to grow crops such as barley and wheat, and raise sheep, goats, cows, and camels.

Eritrea is located in a part of Africa named the Horn of Africa. This area includes the countries of Djibouti, Eritrea, Ethiopia, and Somalia. Eritrea shares borders with Sudan, Ethiopia, and Djibouti.

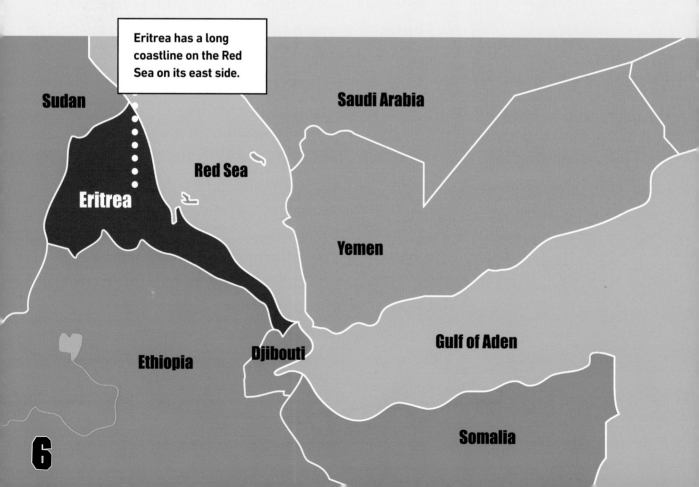

Eritrea has a long coastline on the Red Sea on its east side.

Sudan

Saudi Arabia

Red Sea

Eritrea

Yemen

Gulf of Aden

Ethiopia

Djibouti

Somalia

The colors in Eritrea's flag represent its fight for independence (red), its farming (green), and its long sea coastline (blue).

Eritrea's Story in Numbers

Out of

188

countries ranked, Eritrea is

179th

for its education system, the freedom of its people, and the standard of living.

This street is in Asmara and is part of the central market area. People buy and sell food there.

Asmara is the capital city of Eritrea. Around 800,000 people live there. It has some of Africa's most beautiful historic buildings. It has many wide streets lined with palm trees, and open piazzas, or squares, where people meet. People in Asmara have jobs in industries such as agriculture, making clothing and footwear, and processing meat. Young people may go to one of the universities or colleges there.

Dawit's Story: Growing Up in Eritrea

I grew up with my mother, three brothers, and a sister in a small village called Shambuko. Life for us was always difficult. Mother had a small garden where she grew onions, tomatoes, and **millet**. She ground the millet to make injera, a flatbread that we ate every day.

Mother also kept goats, which gave us milk. She worked hard to make sure we had enough food to eat. But when the rains did not come, our garden dried up and we had little to eat.

This injera is being cooked on a metal tray on a fire.

Many Eritreans keep goats and cows.

Many villages in Eritrea are a long way from the modern capital city, Asmara.

Father had been away since I was four years old. The Eritrean government made him serve in the army. He could only visit us once a year. He used to be very strong. But he became thin and weak. The army treated him badly. They did not give him enough food. Once, when he tried to escape, he was caught and sent to prison. The guards poured hot tea on his legs to punish him. I saw the scars. The army did not pay my father well. He gave my mother most of his money, but it was often not enough for us to buy the food and other things we needed.

I went to school in our village with my brothers. My mother had to pay for us to go there. Sometimes, we were sent home because mother had not been able to pay. Then we had to take turns deciding who could go to school. There was only enough money to pay for one of us.

UN Rights of the Child

You have the right to food, clothing, and a safe place to live.

The Conflict in Eritrea

Ethiopia controlled Eritrea for 20 years. Then, in 1961, Eritrea began its war for independence. This was very difficult because Ethiopia is 20 times bigger than Eritrea.

The war ended in 1991, after 30 years of fighting. The Eritrean army commander was Isaias Afwerki. He became the country's leader and still is today. His government took away the people's rights and freedoms.

The Eritrean and Ethiopian governments are not at peace with one another. Eritrea says that it must defend itself against Ethiopia. It forces its people to serve in the military for this reason. Many Eritrean people are trapped in years and years of military service. They do not get much pay. Many of them try to escape. But when they are caught, they are put in jail or killed.

Isaias Afwerki has been the president of Eritrea for more than 20 years.

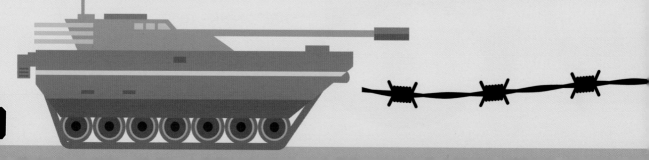

More than

5,000

people flee Eritrea each month to seek safety and freedom in a new country.

The government has made the country **isolated** from the rest of the world. It does not allow many outsiders to visit. Anyone who challenges the government's ideas is put in jail. The country has never allowed its people to vote. The people are powerless to change things. For many, the only hope for a better future is to leave Eritrea.

Many army vehicles, such as this tank, were abandoned after the war with Ethiopia ended. The war cost many lives and millions of dollars.

Dawit's Story: Fleeing Eritrea

When I was 14, my older brother Aman began to talk of leaving Eritrea. He was 17. He would soon have to join the army, like our father. We worried Father might never be free. In a few years, I would be next. Mother decided that Aman and I should escape and go to the Netherlands. Three of our cousins were already there. By traveling together, we could help protect one another.

Many children in Eritrea have grown up knowing nothing but fighting and trouble.

We had to leave secretly. We packed a bag with clothes, some water, and my school notebook. Aman had our cousins' cell phone numbers. Mother gave us money she earned by selling one of our goats. We left late at night and walked until morning. Then we crawled under some bushes and slept until sunset. My belly grumbled as we began to walk again.

It took us four days to walk to the border with Ethiopia. Eritrean soldiers stood guard to stop people from escaping the country. We waited until dark and found a hole in the fence. We tried to sneak through, but the soldiers heard us. They began yelling and shooting. We ran as far as we could, then hid behind a hut until morning.

Some villagers found us. They took us to a place that receives newcomers to Ethiopia. The Ethiopian police were there. They asked us questions about who we were and why we were there. We were sent away in a truck that was traveling to a refugee camp.

Eritrean refugees board buses in Ethiopia. They are then taken to one of the refugee camps in the country.

Fleeing the Conflict

Eritrea has been called "the fastest emptying country on Earth." This is because so many of its people are leaving. Many are teenagers. They are scared of being forced into the army, knowing that they may never be allowed to leave.

The government of Eritrea limits the number of **passports** it will give out. Few people are allowed to leave the country. Anyone caught trying to escape is arrested, put in jail, and beaten. Military police shoot anyone trying to cross the country's borders.

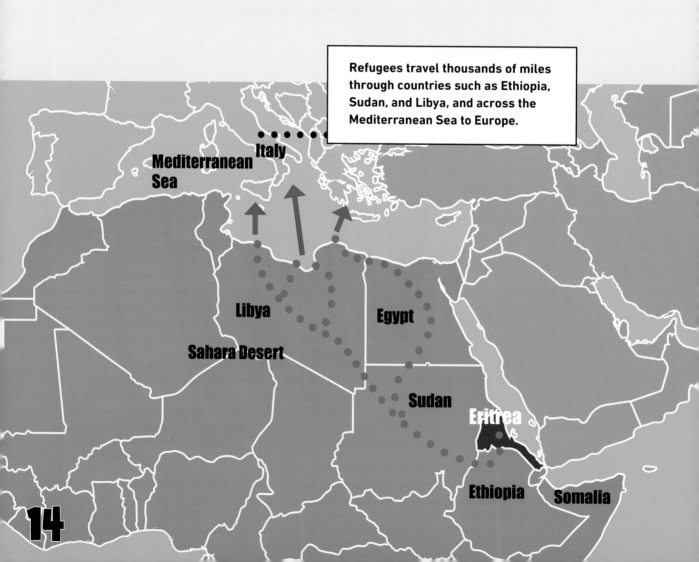

Refugees travel thousands of miles through countries such as Ethiopia, Sudan, and Libya, and across the Mediterranean Sea to Europe.

Italy

Mediterranean Sea

Libya

Egypt

Sahara Desert

Sudan

Eritrea

Ethiopia

Somalia

Eritrea's Story in Numbers

More than

470,000

Eritreans have fled the country.

Temperatures in the Sahara Desert are often above 100°F (38°C) during the day.

The refugees walk across difficult landscapes with only the things that they can carry.

Some refugees flee to camps in Ethiopia or Sudan. Most try to get to Europe. They hope to find better jobs, education, and health care. They follow the world's deadliest **migrant** route through the Sahara Desert and across the Mediterranean Sea.

Many refugees die during the long desert crossing. Others drown crossing the sea in unsafe or overcrowded boats. Many countries they pass through, such as Sudan and Libya, are dangerous. Young refugees are at risk of violence, **human trafficking**, **child labor**, and kidnapping. People who have enough money may pay **smugglers** to help them make the journey. This can cost thousands of dollars—a huge amount of money for the average Eritrean, who earns just $3.50 a day.

Dawit's Story: Life in Adi Harush Camp

Aman and I arrived at a refugee camp named Adi Harush. We shared a one-room hut with four other boys. We slept on dusty mattresses on the floor. A worker at the camp checked on us every day. He made sure we were fed and healthy. Even then, I got **malaria**. I was so sick, I thought I would die. I dreamed of returning home to my mother. But I knew it was too late for that.

Dawit crossed the border into Ethiopia before reaching Adi Harush camp.

Eritrea

Red Sea

Shambuko

Adi Harush

Ethiopia

Aman and I were told we might gain **asylum** in the Netherlands if our cousins sponsored us. This meant they would have to pay for us to go there. We spoke to our cousins from a phone in the camp, and they agreed. The volunteers from the **United Nations High Commissioner for Refugees (UNHCR)** helped us fill out many forms. Months passed, but nothing happened.

Many other refugees were also waiting and hoping to gain asylum, like us. Sometimes, groups of us gathered in someone's hut. We listened to others describe their homeland and how they escaped. They shared news of their journey and the dangers they faced. The journey ahead filled me with fear.

UN Rights of the Child

Children have the right to be protected from kidnapping.
They have the right to be protected from being hurt or mistreated.

Shelter at the refugee camps does not offer much protection from heat and rain.

Eritrean families try to stick together as much as they can. They face a long journey to asylum in Europe.

After six months of waiting, Aman and I were desperate to leave. A smuggler who worked **illegally** in the camp offered to help us escape and make our way to Europe. He wanted us to pay him, but it was far more money than we had. We asked our cousins for help again. They agreed to send the money to the smuggler.

Life in a Refugee Camp

The first stop for many Eritrean refugees is a refugee camp in Ethiopia or Sudan. The UNHCR runs camps that provide food and shelter for more than 150,000 Eritrean refugees. The camps are often crowded and do not have electricity or running water. Many of these camps are in poor countries, which already struggle to care for their own people. They do not have a lot of money to spend helping refugees in camps.

Refugees get their water from wells at the refugee camps.

Different organizations work in the camps to help refugees. For example, Doctors Without Borders provides health care to refugees. The Norwegian Refugee Council offers refugees education and job training. They help refugees learn the skills they need to be independent when they leave the camps.

Refugees carry food and supplies to their homes in the camp.

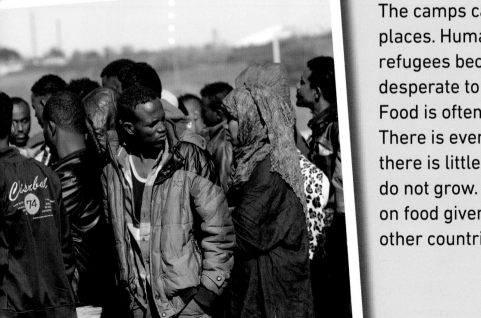

UN Rights of the Child

You have the right to good health care.

Many refugees arrive at the camps hoping to gain asylum in another country and start new lives. But often, they are forced to remain in the camps for years. They must depend on camp workers to survive. The refugees are not allowed to work or go to school outside the camps.

Over the last few years, thousands of refugees have faced starvation in the camps.

The camps can be dangerous places. Human traffickers target refugees because they are often desperate to leave the camps. Food is often in short supply. There is even less food when there is little rain and the crops do not grow. People often survive on food given to the camps by other countries around the world.

Dawit's Story: The Journey to Europe

One day, the smuggler told us to be ready to leave. After everyone went to sleep, we crept out of the camp. We were loaded into the back of a nearby truck. It was already crowded with many others. The smugglers pulled a cover over our heads and the driver sped off.

We drove for days through the desert. During the day, the sun baked us like bread in an oven. My lips cracked and my throat closed from thirst. At night, we shivered in the cold. One day, a woman fell out of the truck when it hit a huge bump on the road. We called out to the driver, but he would not stop. I could not stop thinking about her.

The boats that are used to carry refugees across the Mediterranean Sea are often small and dangerous.

Eritrea's Story in Numbers

More than
3,000
refugees drowned in the Mediterranean Sea in 2016.

Reception centers are short-term homes for the refugees. There, they prepare to continue their journey farther into Europe.

We finally reached the seashore, where they hid us in a warehouse. After dark, we boarded a boat. We were squashed in tightly. There were too many people for the small boat. I was afraid it would sink. The captain guided us out to sea. I shivered as the wind and waves crashed into us. I did not know how to swim. Later, another boat met us to take the captain away. He just left us behind. We had no life jackets, water, or food.

After two days, we saw land in the distance. Another boat brought us to shore. The crew told us we were in Italy. They took us to a warehouse and gave us clean clothes and beds.

Reaching a New Life in Europe

Fewer than 1 in 100 refugees are resettled in Western countries with the help of the UNHCR. Many refugees are forced to find their own way to Europe. Along the way, they must cross country borders. They risk being caught and returned to their homeland.

Those who are successful arrive in southern Europe, often in Italy or Greece. They are taken to **migrant centers**. There, they must complete paperwork to apply for asylum.

Refugees are not prepared for the cold and difficult winters in parts of Europe.

People of all ages are forced to leave their homeland and become refugees.

UN Rights of the Child

You have the right to protection from any kind of **exploitation**.

It can take a long time for refugees to find out if they have gained asylum. They may be sent back to their homeland instead. Most hope to reach countries in northern Europe where there are more jobs and better opportunities.

Only one in four refugees who seek asylum is given the right to stay in Europe. To avoid the risk of being sent home, some refugees stay illegally. They do not apply for asylum. They may end up living on the streets of European cities. Living on the streets is dangerous for refugees. They may be targeted for human trafficking, or forced to join gangs. They often have nowhere to go if they need help.

These asylum seekers prepare to move onward as they leave a migrant center in France.

Dawit's Story: Life in the Netherlands

While we were in Italy, Aman and I were allowed to speak with our cousins in the Netherlands once a week. They wanted to know when we were coming. After two months, we were granted asylum. We traveled by bus to a big city in Italy. A volunteer took us to the train station, where we boarded a train. I had never been on a train before. Things sped past our window so quickly, it made me dizzy.

It can be difficult for refugees to find well-paying jobs in Europe. Many do not have the skills needed, or do not speak the language well enough.

Our cousins were waiting at the train station when we arrived. They took us to their apartment. Aman and I now share a small room. Amsterdam is a big city with many people. It was scary at first. Now I am learning about Dutch food, how to ride the bus, and I am making new friends. I am in a high school class for newcomers. When I understand Dutch well enough, I will join the regular classes.

7 out of 10 Eritreans seeking asylum in Europe are between the ages of **18 and 34.**

I talk to my mother on my cousin's cell phone. We cry when we hear each other's voices. I miss her so much. But she is happy we are safe. Aman is working hard to finish high school. Then he will look for a job. We cannot stay with our cousins forever because their place is too small. Maybe one day, the rest of my family can join us here. I hope so.

Refugee children go to language classes. The classes help them communicate in their new home.

25

Challenges Refugees Face

Canada: 6,500

So many refugees have arrived in Europe. Some countries are finding it difficult to take care of all of them. They want their governments to limit the number of refugees allowed to stay in their country. Some people believe immigrants take their jobs. Others worry that refugees bring violence from their homeland. Many refugees arrive with new attitudes, languages, religions, and food choices. They often face **discrimination**. People worry that refugees are changing their country's way of life.

United States: 84,819

Starting a new life in a country far from home can be lonely and frightening.

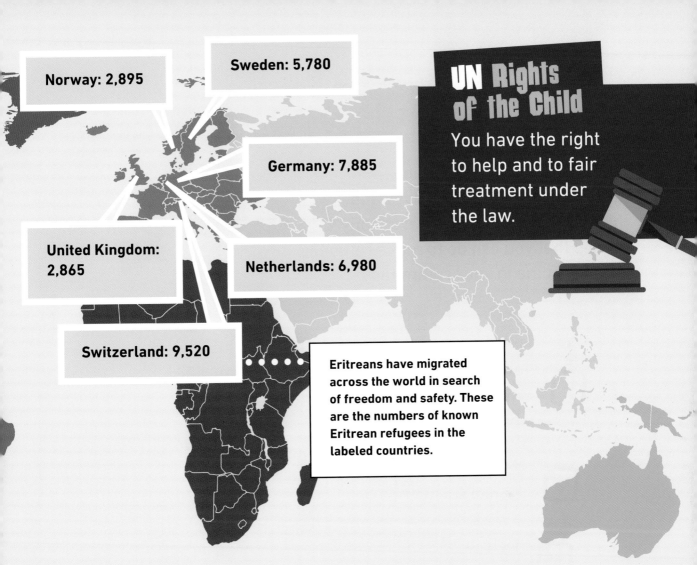

Norway: 2,895

Sweden: 5,780

Germany: 7,885

United Kingdom: 2,865

Netherlands: 6,980

Switzerland: 9,520

UN Rights of the Child

You have the right to help and to fair treatment under the law.

Eritreans have migrated across the world in search of freedom and safety. These are the numbers of known Eritrean refugees in the labeled countries.

It can be very hard for newcomers to adjust to a new language and different beliefs in their new home. They often feel lonely and isolated. Refugee children and young adults who arrive alone are vulnerable. They need help and support to live independently. Adults must learn new skills to find a job. Life can be hard in a new country where things are different.

Refugees who arrive and stay illegally face different challenges. They may be sent back to their homeland if they are caught. They are not protected by the laws in their new country and cannot get support from the government. This means they may not have housing, jobs, or health care.

You Can Help!

It is important to help refugees around the world whose lives and futures are at risk. There are many things that you can do to make refugees feel welcome in your community.

- ☑ Talk about what you have learned in this book with family and friends to raise awareness of the issues that refugees face.

- ☑ Reach out to newcomers arriving in your school to make them feel welcome.

- ☑ Help a newcomer learn English.

- ☑ Take part in a food or clothing drive to support newcomers in your community.

- ☑ Accept an invitation to a newcomer's home to visit, play, or share a meal.

- ☑ Learn more about refugee issues during World Refugee Day every June 20.

- ☑ Encourage your friends to be open and welcoming to newcomers.

UN Rights of the Child

You have the right to practice your own language, culture, and religion.

WORLD REFUGEE DAY

AID

Watch for World Refugee Day events happening each year.

Discussion Prompts

1. Why do so many Eritreans feel they must flee their country?
2. What challenges do refugees face as they start a life in a new country such as the Netherlands?
3. What can your community do to support refugees and newcomers?

Glossary

asylum Protection given to refugees by a country

child labor The illegal use of children to perform work

constitution The document that describes a country's system of beliefs and laws

discrimination The unfair treatment of someone based on gender, race, religion, or other identifiers

exploitation To take unfair advantage of someone

homeland The country where someone was born or grew up

human trafficking When people are smuggled to different countries for money

illegally Against the law

immigrants People who leave one country to live in another

independent Free from outside control

isolated Separated or cut off from other people or places

malaria A disease spread by mosquitoes

migrant A person that travels from one place to another

migrant centers Places that help refugees when they arrive in a new country

military service The time spent serving in a country's army

millet A type of cereal grain

passports Official documents given to citizens by their government that state their identity and eligibility to travel

poverty The state of being very poor and having few belongings

refugees People who flee from their own country to another due to unsafe conditions

rights Privileges and freedoms protected by law

smugglers People who move goods or passengers illegally

United Nations (UN) An international organization that promotes peace between countries and helps refugees

United Nations High Commissioner for Refugees (UNHCR) A program that protects and supports refugees everywhere

Learning More

Books

Milway, Katie Smith. *The Banana-Leaf Ball: How Play Can Change the World.* Kids Can Press, 2017.

NgCheong-Lum, Roseline. *Eritrea* (Cultures of the World). Cavendish Square Publishing, 2011.

Winterberg, Philipp. *Am I Small?* (Bilingual Children's Book English-Tigrinya). CreateSpace Independent Publishing Platform, 2014.

Websites

http://easyscienceforkids.com/eritrea
Discover interesting facts about Eritrea's geography, history, and culture.

www.nationalanthems.info/er.htm
Click the sideways triangle on the right-hand side to listen to Eritrea's national anthem.

www.shabait.com/about-eritrea/erina/16508-eritreas-9-ethnic-groups
Find out about the main ethnic groups in Eritrea.

www.unicef.org/rightsite/files/uncrcchilldfriendlylanguage.pdf
Learn more about the United Nations Convention on the Rights of the Child.

Index

Adi Harush camp 16–17
Afwerki, Isaias 10
Asmara 4, 7, 9
asylum 16, 17, 19, 22–23, 24, 25

challenges 26–27
crops 4, 6, 8, 19

dangers 14–15, 17, 19, 20–21, 23
Dawit's story 8–9, 12–13, 16–17, 20–21, 24–25

education system 7, 9
Ethiopia 5, 6, 10, 11, 13, 14, 15, 18

farm animals 6, 8
finding jobs 15, 18, 23, 24, 25, 26, 27
food shortages 4, 8, 9, 19, 21

government 4–5, 9, 10–11, 14

helping refugees 28–29
host countries 26–27

maps 4, 6, 14, 16, 26–27
Mediterranean Sea crossings 15, 20–21
military service 5, 7, 9, 10, 12, 14

number of refugees 11, 18, 26–27

refugee camps 13, 15–19

smugglers 15, 17, 20–21
staying illegally 23, 27

UN Rights of the Child 5, 9, 13, 17, 19, 23, 27, 29
UNHCR 16, 18, 22

About the Author

Linda Barghoorn studied languages in university because she wanted to travel the world. She has visited 56 countries, taking photographs and learning about different people and cultures. Her father traveled to North America as a German immigrant more than 50 years ago. Linda has written 14 children's books and is writing a novel about her father's life.